THE
AMAZING
WORLD OF
GUMBALL™

MAYHEM
MANUAL

by Mark Shulman and C. Lamison

PSS!
PRICE STERN SLOAN
an Imprint of Penguin Group (USA) LLC

PRICE STERN SLOAN
Published by the Penguin Group
Penguin Group (USA) LLC, 375 Hudson Street, New York, New York 10014, USA

USA | Canada | UK | Ireland | Australia | New Zealand | India | South Africa | China

penguin.com
A Penguin Random House Company

™ and © Turner Broadcasting System Europe Limited, Cartoon Network (s14)

Photo credits: cover and page 1: (#2 pencil, eraser, and ruler) © iStock/Thinkstock; cover and interiors: (crumpled white paper) © koosen/iStock/Thinkstock; (ripped white grid paper) © Robyn Mackenzie/iStock/Thinkstock; (yellow grid paper) © aytac bicer/iStock/Thinkstock; (retro yellow rule paper) © Jayson Gatdula/Hemera/Thinkstock; (ripped yellow rule paper) © Robyn Mackenzie/iStock/Thinkstock; (white grid paper, masking tape, white notebook paper) © Iwona Grodzka/iStock/Thinkstock.

Published in 2014 by Price Stern Sloan, a division of Penguin Young Readers Group, 345 Hudson Street, New York, New York 10014. PSS! is a registered trademark of Penguin Group (USA) LLC. Printed in the USA.

ISBN 978-0-8431-8047-3   10 9 8 7 6 5 4 3 2

Boy, are you lucky!
What do you mean by "lucky," Gumball?
Are you kidding? You get to read this incredible book. MY incredible book. It tells you almost everything you'll ever need to know when it comes to the proper generation and escalation of enjoyable mayhem. It's possibly the best opportunity you'll ever have for ruling the world in world-class style.
That sounds like a lot of work.

COOL
Not if troublemaking comes naturally to you. I mean, I'll show you how to bend rules the way a prisoner bends his window bars.
You realize your example involves prison?
That's ridiculous. The things in this book don't get you arrested. At least, not if you're a kid.
Shouldn't you be including a disclaimer around here?

What? You mean like stating that I, my family and friends, the writers, and my amazing publisher take no responsibility at all for any trouble the average reader might face after trying this brilliant stuff out? You mean blurt out some NONSENSE like that?

YES.

I don't know. I like encouraging people to break the rules. It makes me feel more at home. It also makes me less likely to get in trouble if I can tell Mom: "But everybody's doing it."

You're right, Gumball. I actually am lucky.

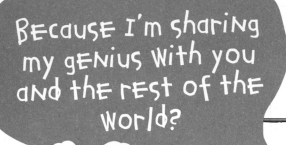

BECAUSE I'm sharing my gENiUS WiTH you and the rest of the world?

NO WAY! I'm lucky that MY NAmE iSN'T ON the front cover.

TABLE OF CONTENTS:

I mEAN, iNVitE the WHOlE class to do it.

Or just kEEP things NEat. likE, don't lEAVE so many sandwichEs UNDEr your bED for thE monstEr.

MONStEr? DarWin, that's it! GEt a monstEr truck and tilt your housE uNtil stuff rolls uNDEr thE bED. BEttEr yEt, flood your WHolE housE.

WatEr just flows out thE door! THE curb Will bE a total mEss. Good thing that's Not your problEm!

How to Cook absolutely anything

Don't like mom's cooking? Don't complain—cook it yourself. Chefs ahoy!

You're not supposed to touch the oven.

It's a microwave. It doesn't even get hot, except when I forget to take out the metal spoon. Mix up seven kinds of pasta with cold cereal, candy, whatever you've got. Toss in french dressing, and you're a french chef. Dig in!

I'M NOT THAT BAD

11

How to Surprise Mom on Her Special Day

Mother's Day isn't fair. It's like Mom gets another birthday, and WE don't!

I NEVER thought of that.

Might as well get her stuff WE like, too. Like fake brains. They're really squishy, and cheap! Or bulldog-riding lessons. After one lesson, she'll let us have the rest.

I heard Mom say she spends all her time working, cooking, and cleaning. Can we help with that?
Washomat
Yes! Let's make a yard sign that says FREE STUFF INSIDE! After everything's been carried off, cleaning will be a snap!
ohyeah!!

Gumball! Let's disguise the phone as a remote. Instead of channel surfing, he'll be ordering a pizza.

Good try, Darwin. But in this case, I think an all-out frontal assault is the only solution. Distract him! Grab it! Eat CARTOONS, Dad!

15

WEll, birds and bEEs, for starters . . .

small detail, DarWiN! I'm advertising our laWN as Earthworm CENtral. By 6:00 a.m. tomorrow, fanatical fishermEN Will dig up the joiNt. No more yard Work!

HOW to HElP With the Laundry

Why is Mom always hassling us about washing our own clothes?

They're filthy, they're smelly . . .

WE can fix that, Darwin. SEE this vile, putrid sock? It's no ordinary vile, putrid sock. It's Cloroxio, the god of laundry. Make a sacrifice—pucker up and kiss him. all our clothes turn lemony-fresh!

THERE must BE another Way.

SurE. Put moths iN our cLOSET. THEy EaT the dirt off the cLOTHES. WE couLD aLSO put DETErgENT iN paiNTbaLL guNS aND bLaST EacH oTHEr cLEaN.

um, WHErE'S that Sock?

ON reality TV! NO NEED to actually bE aNgry. PrEtENd thErE's a camera crEW aNd start Whaling oN Each othEr With fakE hammErs aNd stuff.

That's kiNd of harsh.

FINE. Playing MONOPOLy Would do thE trick, but ONLy if WE gEt to EVict thE losErs. For rEal.

SWEEt! I caN haVE your bEd!

My Family

How to Eat a Whole...
Lot Better

Do you think humans have gone all marshmallowy from poor eating habits?

Have you seen Dad lately?

Worry not! Old Gumball has the million-dollar answer: Exersnacking™! Drop your food on the floor before every bite.

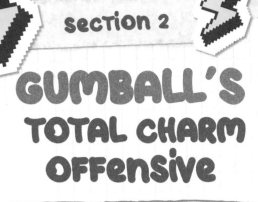

section 2

GUMBALL'S TOTAL CHARM OFFENSIVE

How to Get a Ride to the Mall

The mall is too far away. Why don't kids get to drive?

It's a conspiracy, Darwin. Cars are getting smaller but drivers aren't. We're stuck scamming the adults.

WE could just ask . . .

Oh, like *that* EVER works. No, you have to give Dad a treasure map and *X* is the mall fountain. While he's snorkeling for PENNIES, WE hang out.

Complicated.

Okay, here's an easier way. Pretend a car hits you. On the way to the hospital, just tell the ambulance driver to stop at Burger Barn.

JOYFUL BURGER

25

How to Win, Win, Win at Video Games

Darwin, you are getting sleepy . . . sleeeeeepy . . . now repeat after me:

"Wow, Gumball, you scored 93 million on Mega-Multi-Death-Zapper."

WOW, Gumball. The Earth is 93 million miles from the sun . . .

Rats! It's a good thing hypnotism isn't the only way to get a high game score.

Practice, practice, practice?

Wires, wires, wires. Why waste time perfecting obsolete skills? You can bust open the game console, use an unlock disc, and flip a few switches! Hand me that welding thing, will you?

27

HOW to Dominate the World . . . with Computers!

It's a slow day, Darwin. Let's do a project. Like, maybe, take over the earth!

I dunno, Gumball. That's a lot of work for a slow day.

GUMBALL'S POSITIVE-IMPRESSION MACHINE

HOW to Impress Girls

> Girls don't seem to notice me.

That's because you're a fish, bro. But girls go for pixelated pecs like mine. Know why? Because I burn up the dance floor.

Dancing? Is that what you call those crazy twitches?

You have to be romantic to get the girls, Darwin. Bring 'em flowers. Get 'em jewelry.

I saw PENNY eating that bagel ring you gave her.

You SEE? Sigh! I'm a part of her already . . .

How to upgrade Your Hurting Fashion Style

You should change your clothes, Gumball. They're really getting crusty.

What? Me? I'm not dirty. I'm wearing history. You want to be a hip fashion dude, there's a price to pay.

COOL

32

It's expensive to be fancy.

You can't put a price on style, Darwin. That's why I shop at the lost and found. Check out my bad hat. Want shiny shoes? Put electrical tape on them.

I can't even afford the tape.

If you can't get the clothes, get the fashion magazines, dude. Cut out all the best-looking guys and just wear the pictures!

COOL

33

35

HOW to GEt around TOWN IN StylE

¡yo!

That's it, Darwin. I'm done with walking. From now on, I'm strictly putting on miles with style. Skateboards, scooters . . .

GUMBALL'S COOLER SCHOOLER

HOW to "Do" HomeWork the Effective Way

Sorry, Darwin, there is NO Effective Way to do homework. There are ONLY EFFECTIVE EXCUSES. Let's sing them together.

Dear teacher, I was in the hospital.

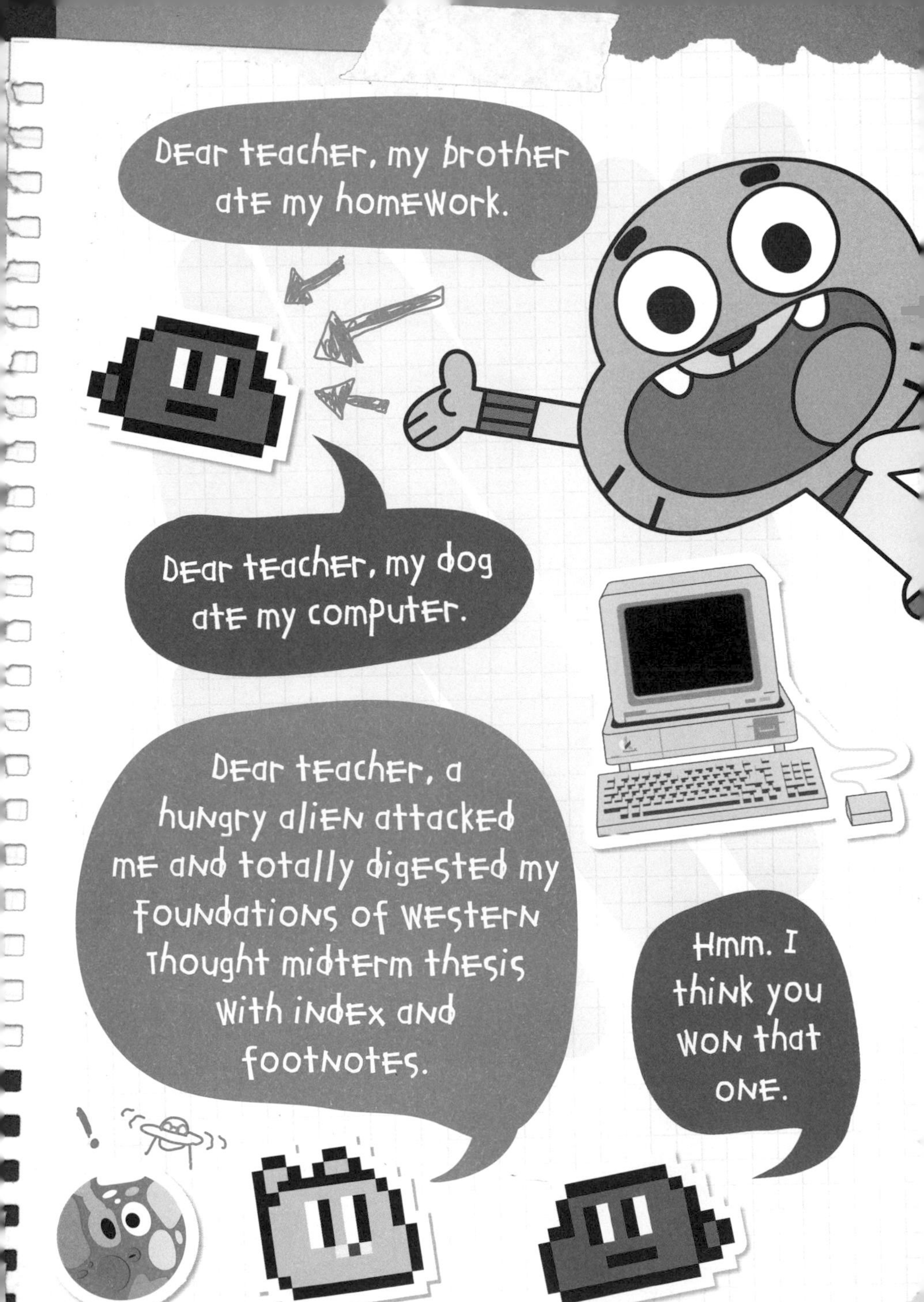
Dear teacher, my brother ate my homework.
Dear teacher, my dog ate my computer.
Dear teacher, a hungry alien attacked me and totally digested my foundations of Western Thought midterm thesis with index and footnotes.
Hmm. I think you won that one.
!

How to avoid School the Effective Way

Why are you sweating homework, Darwin? Today's a school holiday!

Which one?

Thursday. And if you're a Thursday-tarian, you get the day off school.

That's not gonna fly, Gumball.

Ah, don't worry—it was unstable, Darwin. That was bound to happen.

My great ants . . .

Fine. Fine. So I'll give you a backup entry. Here's my super launcher contraption thingy. It can send a ball to the moon.

Sniff. How's *that* going to help me win?

Easy. It'll launch everybody else's projects into space. You'll win by default!

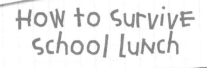

HOW to Survive School Lunch

WE'RE studying the TONG wars in history class.

aWESOME! I heard the Wars WERE bEtWEEN cafeteria PEOPLE. TONGS VERSUS spatulas! TO the finish! and With food that bad, you've got to think like a survivor.

You mEan put lunch trays over our EyES so WE don't have to sEE the chopped-cockroach burgers?

44

That's ONE solution, Darwin. But I was thinking about filling the school-bus engine with the gross, year-old french-fry oil and rocketing away.

So the bus gets the gas instead of us?

Maybe not. For gas, we should probably just get pizzas delivered. Table 11, please.

HOW TO RULE the Classroom

You may have heard that the teacher runs the classroom. Not true.

But I heard it!

Nope, you heard wrong. It's the pupils who have the power.

CHEMISTRY

PHYSICS

46

UNLESS you hit the teacher in her pupil with a paper airplane.

BE CONFIDENT, DARWIN! RIP UP THAT TEST! Your teacher will respect you as a decision maker and future leader . . . no matter how bad your spelling is.

What if I want to express myself as an artist?

That's what the principal's car is for! Think of it as your very own mobile canvas. Spray away!

PLANET EARTH PHYSICS CHEMISTRY DINOSAURS MATHEMATICS BRAIN TRAINING HISTORY BOTANY INTERIOR DESIGN ASTRONOMY MECHANICS

GUMBALL'S WALK OF FAME

HOW to BECOME a TOP MOVIE Star

Hollywood's so last year, Darwin. Here in the Internet era, we post a few memorable videos and we're instant celebrities.

But what should our homemade movie be about?

48

Who cares? As long as we do stupid stunts, we'll get lots of hits. I'll slide down ice-covered stairs. The girls can't get enough.

Get enough what? Ice?

No! Enough thrills from us action-movie stars. All you need is a camera. And the ability to reanimate. And no pain sensors. Zero. And did I mention the cast party?

After the film's done?

No. After the doctor removes the cast. It's a snap!

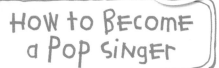

HOW to BECOME a POP SINGER

HEY, Gumball! DON't sing so loud in the shower. The tiles are coming off the walls.

Got to! I'm going to be a pop star on *America's Got No Talent*!

No way! How do you think you're going to win?

I practice EVERYWHERE I can. IN the school hallway. ON the speaker at the CONVENIENCE store. Did you know there are great acoustics UNDER the kitchen sink?

Is that What that NOISE Was? I thought it Was the garbage disposal.

Excuse me, DarWiN. I've got to go soap up my vocal cords. You NEED bubbles to be a POP star!

51

HERE IN the trash can. I'm spying.

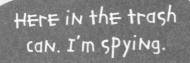

ON Whom?

ON you! But I got bored Waiting for you to NOTICE. It's hard Work beING a spy. You have to be a master of disguise.

You meaN like the time WE came out of that store both WearING makeUP? WE looked like crazy clown girls.

YEah! But spyING is about other things, too. like EXPErt marksmanship. I caN paintball aNyoNE, aNytime, aNyWhErE.

I KNOW. I still have paint iN my Ear.

How to fully Express Yourself artistically

I want to paint something more significant than a garage door. I need one thing . . .

a ruthless art agent?

um, no. Talent.

Darwin, old friend, you don't need talent. You need to be innovative. Garage doors are old technology. Go find a billboard ad and spray your artistic opinion on it. Call it "collage."

I call it "vandalism."

And remember, you can always put down the paintbrush and pick up a paintball gun for a modern touch.

I still have paint in my ear.

GUMBALL'S
SPORTS ADVICE
FOR BAD SPORTS

How to Win a Trophy the Easy Way

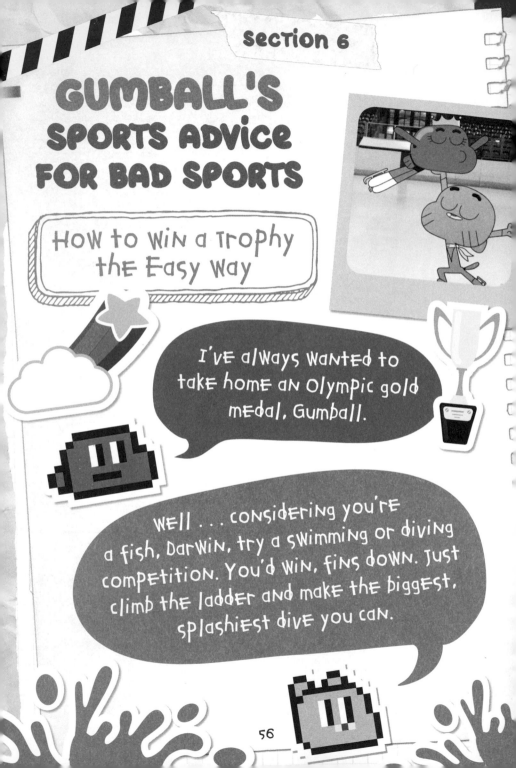

I've always wanted to take home an Olympic gold medal, Gumball.

Well . . . considering you're a fish, Darwin, try a swimming or diving competition. You'd win, fins down. Just climb the ladder and make the biggest, splashiest dive you can.

I'm a little worried about belly flops.

FINE. Practice diving into a mop bucket. Just don't hit the mop.

and that will win me a trophy?

IN my professional opinion, the easiest way to get a trophy is at a yard sale.

Dodgeball. TENNIS ball. The object of the game is not to get hit in the head.

What about a bowling ball?

Especially a bowling ball. REMEMBER: SOME balls are easier to dodge than others!

DUCKS DODGERS

Elmore Rabbits

How to Rule Gym Class—Without Rules!

How'd you get those bruises, Gumball?

They're not bruises! They're my disguise. I'm an undercover star athlete.

DUCKS DODGERS

Elmore Rabbits

You must be pretty deep undercover. I had no idea. Got any advice?

Of course, little bro. For instance, never let go of the football. Even after it's kicked. Even after you land on the goalpost. Hang on.

Sounds painful.

Nah. We pros wear protective gear. Even my T-ball tournaments get pretty rough.

GUMBALL'S SOCIAL CLIMBER'S TOOLS

How to Tell the Truth and Live to Tell about It

Why's mom screaming?

She asked me if her clothes made her look fat.

and you answered her?

REMEMBER, Darwin. The truth isn't scary. Getting in trouble is scary.

You mean like when you set off that stink bomb in class?

Kind of like that. When the truth will get you in trouble, and lying will get you in *more* trouble, there's only one real solution. **RUN!**

63

Effective, but kind of hard to get around school dressed in a trash can.

Good point. Why don't we dress you in a giant vulture suit? Or get a real vulture. If you bully my brother, you will be eaten.

How exactly is this helping?

Got it! We let an actual bull loose in that kid's bedroom. That'll show him what a real bully is.

How to Get along With Your Brother (or Goldfish)

according to SOMEONE ELSE'S grandma, "THE family that plays together stays together." I BELIEVE it. Let's play!

Great idEa. HOW about spitting pEas at Each other? NOW that's fuNNy.

That's NOT fuNNy. GoiNg to thE gym together, gEtting matchiNg mustachEs. HOW about that?

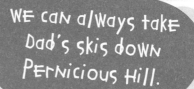

WE can always take Dad's skis down Pernicious Hill.

They're water skis, Gumball.

Exactly!

Let's go!

67

GUMBALL'S DEPARTMENT OF HEALTH

Oral Hygiene—How to Brush and Rush (But Never Have to One Day Eat Mush)

Elio's CHEWING GUM

ask Dr. Gumball: There's only one way to effectively brush your teeth. And that way is . . . to outsource the job.

No way. I'm not brushing *your* teeth!

68

Climb in, Darwin. I'll give you some candy . . .

Okay. all done. Now will you brush my teeth?

No Way. That's disgusting.

That's okay. I didn't give you toothpaste, anyway. I used Dad's deodorant soap.

u/p!

HOW to Make Bath Time Fun—Yes, FUN!

Dude, after a long day of wrestling old ladies at the supermarket, I like to relax by juggling onions and blue-cheese balls.

Please go take a bath, Gumball. My eyes are melting. I'm dying here.

I'm sort of against traditional baths, you know. I think humans should create mutant ants that eat all the food stains and other dirt on our bodies.

Cough. Cough. Gag. If you don't take a shower, I'm going to drag you in myself.

That really stinks, Darwin.

You have no idea.

71

according to my dictionary, that mEANS you control light and sound for slEEping during the daytime. HOW do you do that?

By pulling the covers over my head.

and if that doESN't Work?

I go to the hospital and slEEp there. They'vE got ElEctric multiposition bEds. You can slEEp in any dirEction you WaNt!

GUMBALL'S MONEY-MAKING MISCHIEF

HOW to BE aN UNForGETTABLE BABySITTER

You KNOW the BEST thing about having a kid sister or brother? GETTING paid to babysit!

shouldN'T WE do it for love and family?

74

LOVE and family don't buy the candy bars. BE firm but commanding with that SWEET little devil. USE the most important tool.

affection?

a leash. Especially on the younger ONES. and Not just for transportation. any game in which you tie up the kid could work.

DIDN'T you try that ON ME ONCE?

LISTEN, if you don't KEEP a grip on the little thugs, they'll suck out your EYEballs. They're . . . they're . . . IS that baby looking at ME??? NO!

75

HOW to Make Cash Off the Neighbors

anytime Mom and Dad close the Bank of Mom and Dad, you don't have to look far to replace the lost income. MONEY! That's what NEighbors are for.

That's what NEighbors are for?

Positively! You can help them in so many ways: Clean their car. For money. Feed them lunch. For money. Clip their toenails. For money.

What if they say no?

Why ask? Just do the odd jobs they don't EVEN KNOW they WANT DONE. For instance, lying in front of their doorway to KEEP skunks from coming in. THEN SEND them a bill.

What if they WON'T pay?

RELAX. THEY'RE NEIGHBORS. I KNOW WHERE they stash their money.

HOW to Earn a Living as a Bounty Hunter

I Wish WE had ENough moNEy to rENt The History of ViolENt MoViES, Part IV.

DON't dESPAir, DarWiN. WE'VE got EVErythiNg WE NEEd right HErE to EarN PlENty of MoNEy.

a WaNtEd PostEr? HOW do you thiNk WE'rE goiNg to fiNd a CONVENiENCE-storE robbEr?

We can lurk around a store and ask the owners if they've got any suspicious customers lurking around their store.

That will bring us money?

Or get us arrested. Then we can sue for false arrest and have *plenty* of money to rent the whole series!

HOW to GEt a JOb as a ChEf

NOt fEEling uP to bEing a babysitter or doormat to gEt sPENding moNEy? ThEN lEt's ExplorE a lifE iN food sErvicE. I just wENt shopping iN a vEry high-class garbagE caN.

I'll usE thE Eggs aNd practicE making a soufflé. Oh No! ThErE arE chicks coming out of thEsE Eggs!

NEvEr miNd. Did you kNow you caN sErvE moldy mEat aNd it tastEs EvEN bEttEr than "frEsh"? It's thE Extra protEin.

What's iN that caN? It doEsN't havE a labEl.

LabEls doN't mattEr. If somEbody carEd ENough to caN it, I carE ENough to sErvE it to paying customErs. I'll opEN it.

WhEw! I'm glad it's oNly a rat. I was afraid it might bE brussEls sprouts.

BBQ SAUCE